Anonymous

Life of Saint Bernard

SALZWASSER
VERLAG

Anonymous

Life of Saint Bernard

Reprint of the original, first published in 1858.

1st Edition 2023 | ISBN: 978-3-37515-284-0

Verlag (Publisher): Salzwasser Verlag GmbH, Zeilweg 44, 60439 Frankfurt, Deutschland
Vertretungsberechtigt (Authorized to represent): E. Roepke, Zeilweg 44, 60439 Frankfurt, Deutschland
Druck (Print): Books on Demand GmbH, In de Tarpen 42, 22848 Norderstedt, Deutschland

LIFE

OF

SAINT BERNARD,

FOR CHILDREN

FROM EIGHT TO TEN YEARS OLD.

LONDON:

RICHARDSON AND SON, 147, STRAND;

9, CAPEL STREET, DUBLIN; AND DERBY.

MDCCCLVIII.

TO

THE MOTHER OF THE MOTHERLESS,

THE SUPERIORESS OF THE

CATHOLIC ORPHANAGE AT KENSINGTON,

THIS LITTLE STORY IS DEDICATED

WITH FEELINGS OF THE

DEEPEST RESPECT AND ADMIRATION

FOR THE ADMIRABLE MANNER

IN WHICH SHE TRAINS THE CHILDREN WHOM

PROVIDENCE HAS COMMITTED

TO HER TENDER CARE.

LIFE OF ST. BERNARD.

CHAPTER I.

Grandmamma. Now my little boy I will tell you the story I promised to relate, if you were very good and attentive to your lessons.

Elizabeth. A true story, dear Grandmamma—pray let it be something which has really happened.

George. Yes, and about a boy, Grandmamma; I never like stories concerning little girls, or their dolls. I am to be a man, and I like to hear about boys and men best, of course.

Grandmamma. I am glad that my story will just suit you, it is the life of a most excellent little boy who grew to be a still more perfect man, the great St. Bernard.

Elizabeth. I thought that was the name of a mountain in Switzerland, not of a human being.

Grandmamma. And you are right, my love; but the mountain was named after the man.

George. The story—the story, Grandmamma—don't begin a lesson in geography, I have had one already this morning.

Grandmamma. Elizabeth, daughter of Count Bernard de Montbar, married in early youth, Técelin Lord or Seigneur de Fontaines, near Dijon. She was only fifteen when she left her father's roof to manage her husband's family, and though youthful, she was such a pious, steady well behaved lady, that she soon made her house an example for the surrounding neighbourhood. Elizabeth had six sons and one daughter; Guido was the eldest, then Gerard, Bernard, André, Barthélemi, Nivard, and Hombeline, their little sister. Bernard, whose life I am going to relate, was born in 1091.

George. I wish I could remember the date, Grandmamma.

Grandmamma. So you will, my dear boy; recollect it is just twenty-five years after the conquest of England by the Normans.

Elizabeth. What a lucky thought of yours, dear Grandmamma!—now we shall feel more at home with little Bernard, knowing that he was born when William the Conqueror reigned.

Grandmamma. Bernard's Mamma taught all her children to endeavour to overcome any faults in their temper, or disposition; she also taught them by her example to deny themselves any little pleasure which could be purchased with money, and to give the amount to the poor. Bernard loved his kind good Mamma, with all the strength of his affectionate little heart; he used to go on his knees several times during the day, in his own room, and when his nurse asked why he did so, he answered "to pray like dear Mamma;" he also gave bread to poor children "because dear Mamma did so;" he rendered all sorts of little services to his brothers and to all who approached him, trying as far as his age permitted, to live like his mother; he was a very silent little boy, yet, of course he sometimes did naughty things, and when it happened that he had been in fault, he would steal away to his own room, and there kneeling by the side of his little bed, Bernard would weep and sob out a childish prayer to the Almighty for forgiveness.

George. Oh! Grandmamma, what a nice good little boy; how I wish I could do the same.

Grandmamma. So you can, my darling—even little Bernard did not find it easy at first; but each time he mastered a fault, it was like you in the garden pulling up the gooseberry bush; the first time you tried, it was very hard work, the roots were strong and deep, and George grew very red in the face, and was going to give it up, then Grandmamma called out, " One more strong pull, George; don't give in;" then you gave another, and we heard one root crack in the ground; that gave you courage and made the bush loosen; another pull and another, and up came the little shrub, and George with his face in a glow, felt that perseverance made him conquer a difficulty. Thus it is with our faults, my child; the first battle is the hardest, but every time we struggle to master them, we crack a root of the gooseberry bush.

George. Capital! dear Grandmamma; every time I long to be naughty, if I do not give way, I shall break a root of the gooseberry bush:—but now some more about the good little boy.

Grandmamma. Bernard, at a very early age, was remarkably fond of learning, and remembered his lessons with quickness and ease. His little face was ever smiling with that innocent joy so attractive in a child. His hair was golden ; his complexion very fair, and his figure slender. His face was the face of his father, but his heart and soul were those of his gentle mother, the Dame de Fontaines. An event now occurred which had a great effect on little Bernard's fate. He was in church on Christmas Eve, seated waiting quietly and patiently for the commencement of the Divine Office. It was late for a child to be out of his bed, and Bernard's little head dropped lower and lower on his bosom, and at last he fell fast asleep. While he slept he had either a dream, or a vision, of our blessed Saviour as a new born Infant, more lovely than any child ever was, before or since; He looked on the face of the Incarnate Word made flesh, and when he awoke he told his mother what he had seen, and from that moment a kind of change came over Bernard, and he seemed to devote himself more entirely to the service of that Saviour whose beautiful countenance he always believed he saw in his vision on Christmas Eve. Bernard was sent to school at Chatellon sur Seine, where he learned to read and write Latin with ease, and became exceedingly fond of study.

George. Grandmamma I am afraid I shall never be like Bernard. I am afraid I like play much better than lessons.

Grandmamma. I dare say you do my child, but remember what I said just now of the gooseberry bush.

George. So I will, dearest Granny; and I will give it a good pull to-morrow morning in the school-room.

Elizabeth. So will I, dear Grandmamma; we will have up all the bushes by their roots.

Grandmamma. That is easier said than done, my children; but you must each settle what fault you mean to attack first, and leaving the others for a future day, never cease fighting that which you have selected, until you have conquered it. When

Indians go to battle they each choose an enemy as a mark for their arrows; for if they shot indiscriminately at the advancing body of their foes, they would not kill half the number. Thus it is with our foes too; and no Indian is half so dangerous to a christian as his own sins: if we resolve to vanquish them *all*, we shall make little progress; but by taking them one by one, we shall manage them with greater ease, and by degrees we shall, as Elizabeth says, "have all the bushes up by the roots." But we are forgetting little Bernard at Chatellon, busily employed with his lessons. His elder brothers both became soldiers, which was a sad grief to the Dame des Fontaines, who loved her children dearly; but in those days, there was but one profession which noblemen followed, they became Knights, or led their own peasants to battle. Guido and Gerard were called to the camp of the Duke of Burgundy. The eldest was a grave young man, very modest and retiring, but with a sound judgment;—Gerard's manners were simple and unpretending, he possessed great prudence and presence of mind. Bernard now returned home, having finished his studies at Chatellon; he was nineteen years of age, tall, well formed, with the same sweet expression of countenance for which he was famed as a little child. Six months afterwards a sorrow fell on him, which put an end to all his home happiness. His dear excellent mother died suddenly, and the circumstances of her death are so touching that I must tell them to you.

Elizabeth. Oh! do, Grandmamma. Poor Bernard, how sorry I am for him, he never could have been happy again.

Grandmamma. Dear Elizabeth, he knew that it was God's wish to take his mother to the joys of heaven, and though he grieved deeply for a loss

nothing can replace, yet as time went on he was
comforted, knowing that she was far happier than
on earth; but I must tell you more about the admirable Dame de Fontaines. She was often seen
alone and on foot, on the road from Fontaines to
Dijon, entering the houses of the poor, visiting the
sick, and giving them medicine and food, and what
was still more christian, she used to go to them
without a servant, that no one might know all
the good she did. She was in the habit of invit-
ing all the clergy on the feast of St. Ambrose, the
patron of the church of Fontaines, to a grand
dinner, and to the astonishment of her family, she
announced to them a day or two previously, that
the hour of her death was at hand, she should die
on St. Ambrose's feast. They soon found, however,
that there was great cause for fear, as on the vigil
she was attacked by fever which obliged her to keep
her bed; on the morning of the feast she humbly
requested that the Blessed Sacrament might be given
to her, and having received this Holy Viaticum,
together with Extreme Unction, she felt strengthened, and desired that the Ecclesiastics should sit
down to the banquet prepared for them. While they
were at dinner, Elizabeth de Fontaines sent for
Guido, the eldest son, and commanded him, as soon
as the repast was over, to bring all the Clergy into her
room. She then declared that the moment of her
death was at hand. The astonished priests commenced the Litanies, which she sang with them as
long as her breath lasted, but at the words " by thy
Passion and Cross, deliver us, O Lord," the dying
christian raised her hand to make the sign of salva-
tion, and expired in that attitude.

George. Explain that to me, Grandmamma; what
does it mean?

Grandmamma. My child, she raised her hand to make the sign of the cross, and died with her hand in that position, to the great surprise of all present.

Elizabeth. What an extraordinary thing, dear Grandmamma!

Grandmamma. Yes, my love, but the whole life of Elizabeth de Fontaines was as unlike that of ladies in general as her death ; she was a Saint, and a fitting mother for so glorious a son.

Elizabeth. Dear Grandmamma, will you be so good as to tell me exactly what you mean when you say a person is a Saint ; I have heard many people use that word, and they all seem to have a different idea in their minds; will you tell me what makes a Saint?

Grandmamma. First tell me, my dear child, your own feeling on the subject.

Elizabeth. I think a Saint is born perfect, a person who never commits sin, never makes God angry, and I suppose there are never any Saints now.

Grandmamma. My child, your idea of a Saint is that of many people much older, but not much wiser than my little girl; Saints are born with all our own tendency to sin, but they have one blessing which brings all others in its train ; they love God better than anything in this world: the effect of this affection is, that they will suffer anything sooner than make Him angry, and as nothing but sin has that effect, hence their constant endeavour not to commit it, or if through weakness they do anything wrong, they immediately beg His pardon, and ask for strength not to offend Him again.

Elizabeth. Why, Grandmamma, then there is nothing to prevent any one being a Saint.

Grandmamma. Excepting the infirmities of our nature, and not having sufficient love of God; that

was not Bernard's case; he truly and deeply loved
his heavenly Father, and he grieved with grief too
deep for words, for the loss of his gentle mother—he
was like one stunned; he had just arrived at the age
when a child understands the real, the priceless value
of a mother; in early youth we love them by instinct,
but as we grow older we see each year more vividly,
that the first, truest, and best friend this world will
ever give us, is her on whose bosom our infant head
softly nestled.   Bernard heard her voice no more; no
longer could he watch at the great gate for the first
glimpse of her figure, returing from the village of
Fontaines, on her charitable errands; he had lost the
best part of himself, and he was for a time crushed
by the blow.   The Seigneur Técelin de Fontaine
urged Bernard to choose some settled mode of life,
and one day when he was riding to Dijon to see his
brothers, feeling very wretched, a voice in his heart
seemed to repeat those beautiful words of our
blessed Saviour, "take my yoke upon you and
you shall find rest for your souls."   He was greatly
moved, and passing a church door, he knelt before
the altar, and prayed to God with many tears to
guide him in whatever way He wished him to go : a
calm fell on his soul, and he determined to give up
the honours of this world, of which we are so soon
deprived by death, and to choose that heavenly
crown which is not won without many struggles,
but lasts for eternity.

George. Dear Grandmamma, do not use such
long words: tell me what all that means.

Grandmamma. I was then speaking more to
your Sister, my dear; and I forgot you; but always
tell me if you do not understand, and I will explain
in *little* words more suited to your age. It means
that Bernard did not wish to be a rich, great

man in this world, but to be a good man, and go to Heaven to be with God for ever. So Bernard determined that he would not enter the army, like his brothers, but that he would become a Priest, and work for God and the poor. This was a vexation to the Seigneur Técelin de Fontaines, who wished to see his sons become good soldiers like himself; but Bernard talked so much, and so well, to all his family, showing them how foolish it is to think of this short life, instead of that which is to come, and will have no end, that his uncle, the valiant Count de Trouillon, and his brother Barthélemi both determined to follow Bernard's example, and devote themselves to God's service. Andrew, a younger brother, would not listen to him, and was very cross and angry when Bernard asked him to give up the world; but one day he ran to Bernard with tears in his eyes, exclaiming that he too would join him now. Guido, the eldest brother, though married, next resolved to give up the world ; but to do this he must obtain the consent of his young wife, as they were ever after to live separated from each other. The poor lady, who loved her husband dearly, refused to allow Guido to leave her ; but Bernard talked to her so earnestly that at last half dead with sorrow and illness she consented.

Elizabeth. Was it right of Guido, Grandmamma, to wish to leave his wife, and make her so wretched?

Grandmamma. No, my dear, I do not think it was. If he meant to be a Priest, he should not have married; and being married he should not wish to be a Priest. Guido's wife afterwards became a nun in the convent of Juilly, and at last she was abbess there for some years. Gerard de Fontaines was greatly displeased at the extraordinary events in his family, and Bernard went to see him at the camp at Grancey, when Gerard received him very coldly. Bernard talked to him, as he had done to the others, of the folly of preferring the happiness of this life to the unending peace of the next world; Gerard was not in the least moved by his arguments, and determined not to leave the army, where his courage and prudence were so much esteemed. Then Bernard placed his hand on his brother's side and exclaimed in a prophetic tone,

" Gérard, I know well that nothing but sorrow and pain will open thine eyes to the truth. The day will come, and that soon, when this spot which I touch will be pierced by a lance, which will open a way for my words to reach thy heart."

Gérard afterwards said that while Bernard spoke he felt as if a lance really pierced his side, and what is still more curious a few days afterwards, at the siege of the castle of Grancey, he was wounded by a lance in the very part his brother had touched.

Elizabeth. How very extraordinary, Grandmamma. Why that is being a prophet!

Grandmamma. You will hear of more wonderful things than that, in the life of St. Bernard, my child.

George. Go on, dear Grandmamma. I want to know if Gérard died of his wound.

Grandmamma. Poor Gérard fell senseless on the field of battle, and the enemy took possession of him, and carried him prisoner to their camp. In this sad condition, believing himself dying, Gérard sent for Bernard, wishing to bid him adieu. Bernard, however, would not go, but sent a message to this effect, " Thy wound will not kill, but give thee life,'' meaning that it would make him think more about Heaven, and study the means of getting there. Gérard escaped from his prison, and then determined to become a Religious like the rest of his brothers. Bernard's company now numbered thirty young men of the best families in France; all wearing the dress suited to their rank, but leading a life of prayer, meditation and good works. It became necessary to choose the order of monks to which they should belong, and the choice of Bernard fell on the Cistercian monastery of Citeaux, the most severe rule then existing.

Elizabeth. Oh! how terrible—was it not enough to give up every comfort in the world, without choosing such a desert as a home, and such severities?

Grandmamma. My dear little girl, Bernard was not a man of half measures, the only home he cared for was Heaven, and the shortest and surest way of arriving there, was the road best suited to his taste.

George. Do the Cistercians give themselves the discipline, Grandmamma? I should not like that much, it is as bad as being flogged at school.

Elizabeth. No, not half, you silly little brother; you do not flog yourselves, do you, at school? I think it would not be so hard as the master's whipping.

George. True, Sissy, I had not thought of that difference; I wish they would bring in the fashion at our school, that we should flog ourselves; they were clever men those good old monks.

Grandmamma. My boy, I am afraid you would find the discipline of the Cistercian monks even less to your taste than those unmentionable twigs of birch: the severity with which they treated their bodies would be astonishing to your English ears in this century of self-indulgence.

George. Well, dearest Granny, what happened to Bernard when they arrived at Citeaux?

Grandmamma. Before they went thither, they

all repaired to Fontaines, to ask their father's blessing and bid him adieu. Poor old Técelin was nearly broken-hearted, and their sister, Hombeline, wept sadly and intreated her brothers not to leave their house and relations, but nothing could alter their resolution. As they passed through the court-yard of the castle of Fontaines, they saw their little brother, Nivard, at play with some children of his own age. Guido called him, and taking the boy in his arms, said,

"My dear little brother, do you see this castle and these broad lands? they will be yours, and yours alone."

"What," replied little Nivard, "you take Heaven for yourselves, and leave me this piece of the earth—the division is not equal."

From this time nothing could restrain the child, he would go with Bernard and his brothers that he might earn a corner in Heaven as well as those he loved so dearly.

Elizabeth. What became of the poor old father?

Grandmamma. Some years afterwards the aged Técelin rejoined his sons, and died in the arms of Bernard.

George. How did they go to Citeaux, Grandmamma?

Grandmamma. They all journeyed together on foot, Bernard walking at their head. This was in the year 1113.

CHAPTER II.

George. Now, dear Grandmamma, I have commenced pulling up one gooseberry bush, this morning; therefore I hope you mean to tell us how Bernard and poor little Nivard liked Citeaux when they arrived. I pity the poor child, walking all that distance, he must have felt so tired, and wished he had not left Fontaines.

Grandmamma. Let us wait a few minutes, my dear little boy, until Elizabeth has finished her music and then we will follow Bernard to the monastery; in the meantime I should like to hear which of your faults you began endeavouring to conquer this morning.

George. Why, dearest Granny, you know I dislike my lessons *very, very* much, and of all the lessons, I think the Latin one the most disagreeable. So thought I to myself, this is a gooseberry bush, I will give it a pull. How do you think I did it, Grandmamma?

Grandmamma. Indeed, my child, I cannot guess, but I am very much pleased to hear that you did anything towards conquering your distaste for study.

George. I construed two whole lines more than I had been desired ; was not that a pull, Granny ?

Grandmamma. Yes, my good little boy, it was, and you were rewarded first, by feeling you had done right; you are rewarded again by seeing how much you have pleased me; but the third reward is the greatest and best, you pleased Almighty God, who sees all your little thoughts, and your childish actions, and never fails to recompense or punish,

2

according to our deserts; remember that however dearly Grandmamma loves her boy, our kind Father in Heaven loves him better still.

George. But I can see you, Granny, and I cannot see my Heavenly Parent, that makes *such* a difference.

Grandmamma. My child, reflect a little; you cannot see the air you breathe, yet you know it is around you on every side, wherever we may travel, from the equator to the pole, still the same invisible air surrounds us, we could not live for a moment without it. In the same manner the Spirit of God is about all His creatures; we cannot see Him either, but we know He is present.

George. Yes, I understand; but when I am naughty I forget that God is near, and sees me.

Grandmamma. We all do, my darling, if we recollected the presence of God, we should none of us ever be wicked:—but here comes Elizabeth, and we will continue the life of Bernard; we left him, I think, on the road to Citeaux; but first I must give you an idea of the place to which he was going.

The order of Citeaux was founded by Robert, the holy abbot of Molesme, in the year 1100. He revived the rule of St. Benedict in all its severity. Citeaux was a sort of desert in the dark forests of Beaume in Burgundy; it was governed by Stephen Harding, an Englishman of noble birth. A disease had ravaged the country all round, and the poor monks suffered severely, for the life they led was so hard, that the religious of other orders spoke of Citeaux with a shudder. Thus, when attacked by the fever, they had no strength to resist it, and numbers died, which made the abbot very unhappy, for he thought that the order would die with the few sickly monks who still lived. One day they were all at prayer, when they saw a troop of men with a young man at their head, slowly cross an opening in the forest, and stop at the entrance to the monastery. You can guess whom they were.

George. Poor little Nivard, I hope they did not make him practise austerities too.

Grandmamma. They all began their novitiate at once; but Bernard being delicate soon fell ill, and had long fainting fits; whatever he ate made him sick, and he could scarcely sleep at all. The monks divided their time between hard work in the forest and prayer; they cut down the trees, cleared the ground, and prepared it for crops. Bernard could not cut down trees, but he learned to chop wood and carry it; he became very fond of being in the wild forest, where he studied the works of God; it was there, he said, that he learned to understand the Holy Scriptures, " that the oaks and beeches of the forest taught him."

Elizabeth. What did he mean, Grandmamma?

Grandmamma. He meant that he studied God's ways, in the wonderful works of nature. Nothing is more astonishing than a tree in full leaf. First, it is held fast in the ground, by long arms, that wind their way through the soil, and at the end of these long arms are little invisible mouths, which select the proper juices that suit each species of tree, and suck them first through the little fine roots, into the great roots, and from the great roots up the huge trunk, then through all the branches, at last forming leaves and flowers. How unlike is the lovely Magnolia, with its pure white petals, and delicate smell, to the drops of mud-coloured moisture that were first sucked in by the roots of the tree, and then changed, God alone knows how, into the beautiful blossom we admire so much!

Elizabeth. I never thought of that before; how silly of me. Why roses and carnations are made of mud, by some wonderful change in the stem of the plant: no wonder Bernard said he was taught by the trees.

Grandmamma. The example of St. Bernard was followed by such numbers of young men, that the Abbot thought it necessary to form a second monastery and then a third; the latter was in a marshy piece of forest in the province of Langres. To this place Bernard's brothers, his uncle, and some other monks, twelve in all, were sent, St. Bernard being placed at their head. The ceremony observed on these occasions was simple and touching; the Abbot of the mother house placed a cross in the hands of him who had been chosen to head the new colony, then the new Abbot bade adieu to his brethren, and carrying the cross, followed by the monks who were to go with him, they all left the church. Tears streamed from the monks' eyes as St. Bernard left them, and though they tried to sing a hymn, it finished in a sob. They walked sometimes through a barren country, sometimes through thick forests, until they came to the swampy valley which was to be their future home; it was called the valley of wormwood, Clara Vallis, but St. Bernard named it Clairvaux. Clairvaux had been a celebrated haunt for robbers, and the country people were so glad to have the good monks for neighbours instead of the banditti, that they helped St. Bernard and his companions to clear the ground, and to build their little cells. They soon however fell into great distress, for being always building they could not till their land, and with great difficulty they managed to get a little barley or millet, with which they made bread, having nothing to eat but the leaves of beech trees, cooked in salt and water.

Elizabeth. George, do you remember when the cook forgot to make our currant pudding the other day, how angry we were, and how ill used we thought ourselves?

George. Yes, Sissy, and I had two helps of roast mutton and potatoes. I wonder what St. Bernard would have thought of us? The next time it happens, I shall remember his dinner on boiled beech leaves.

Grandmamma. But that was not all; what do you think, George? One day their salt failed them.

George. What! beech leaves without salt? why that must be as nasty as Senna tea! Poor monks! I hope they were not starved to death.

Grandmamma. When they told St. Bernard there was no salt, he called one of the monks and said: "Guibert, my son, take the ass, and go to buy some salt in the village."

"My Father, will you give me some money to pay for it?"

"Have confidence," said St. Bernard, "there is One above who keeps my purse, and takes care of our treasures."

Guibert smiled and replied, "My Father, if I go empty handed, I fear I shall return empty handed."

"Go still," said St. Bernard, "and go with confidence." Upon this order Guibert saddled the ass, and went to the market; not far from the town, he met a Priest, who asked him from whence he came. Guibert told him that he was going to market without money to buy salt for the beech leaves. This simple answer so touched the Priest's heart, that he took him to his house, and gave him a quantity of provisions. The happy Guibert returned in haste to his hungry brothers, and throwing himself at St. Bernard's feet, related what had happened.

"I told thee so, my son," said St. Bernard; "there is nothing more necessary to be a christian, than confidence in God: never lose it, and it shall be well for thee all the days of thy life."

Elizabeth. What a beautiful speech, Grandmamma.

Grandmamma. Yes my love, full of the spirit of true Christianity, and as well suited to us in the 19th century, as it was to Guibert in the 12th. If we really and truly trusted in the goodness of the Almighty, one great source of worldly sorrows would be at once cut off, we should never fret ourselves about our future fate in this life, trusting it wholly in the hands of Him, who loves us so much, that He allowed His Son to perish by a lingering death, to win the pardon of our sins.

George. Did they continue to eat beech leaves, Grandmamma?

Grandmamma. No, my child; when once their poverty was known, relief came from all sides, and St. Bernard soon had the comfort of seeing his monastery flourish: the monks still continued to live in little huts, round their church, and St. Bernard became so ill that for a year he was not able to manage the affairs of the order. A doctor was sent for, who was a very ignorant stupid man, and his medicines made St. Bernard much worse; however, he obeyed the quack's directions, and suffered cruelly from them. One day a friend, William de St. Thierry, came to see him, and to enquire how he felt,

"Happy—perfectly happy," replied St. Bernard; "but before I was ill, reasonable men obeyed me, and now I am sick, I obey a man without any reason,"—meaning the doctor.

Elizabeth. Grandmamma, forgive me for interrupting you, but are there, any monasteries of St. Bernard's order now?

Grandmamma. Yes, my love, there are many on the Continent,—not forgetting St. Bernard's monastery near Loughborough in Leicestershire. Bernard recovered from his illness; and resumed the severity with which he treated himself, and the gentle kindness with which he treated every other person, with even greater zeal than before he suffered from his disease. One day several knights, on their way to a tournament, passed by Clairvaux, and asked a night's lodging in the monastery. It was towards the end of Lent, and Bernard, while he showed every attention and hospitality to the travellers, told them that he was sincerely sorry to see Christian gentlemen amusing themselves in such a manner, at a season when the church is occupied with prayer and fasting; " I only ask you to put off the tournament until after Easter," said the holy man to his guests: but they were young and wild, and would not give up their amusement, even at the request of one whose holy life and excellent writings had made him celebrated throughout Europe.

" You will not grant my request, noble knights," said Bernard in his kindest accents.

No answer: they could not refuse, and they would not agree to what he wished.

" In that case, I shall ask it of God, and I have a firm confidence that *He* will not refuse me."

He then ordered wine to be set before them, blessed the cup, and said, " drink, noble knights, to the better health of your souls."

They drank, and afterwards took leave of the good Abbot; but they had not ridden far, when each began comparing the useless life of pleasure which he led,

with the holy lives of the monks they had just quit-
ted; every hour bringing its appointed employment,
and every employment having for its object either
the good of their souls, or the advantage of their
neighbours ; presently the knights began talking
to each other, of what was the subject of their
thoughts; one more excited than the rest exclaimed,
" Let us return to him."

" Yes, yes," cried the others, and all the horses'
heads were turned towards Clairvaux.

They stripped off their armour, and laid it at
Bernard's feet, asking him to receive them among
his sons, and gave up the rest of their lives to the
peaceful exercise of Christian virtues.

Elizabeth.   How very wonderful l that must have
been the effect of Bernard's prayer.

Grandmamma.   Of course it was, my dear; did
not our blessed Saviour say to sinners even, " Ask
and ye shall receive?" how much more probable that
He should grant the prayer of a good holy man,
whose whole life was passed in the service of his
Lord.

Clairvaux became much too small to contain the
crowds of men of all ranks, who were attracted by
the reputation of holiness and sanctity of St. Bernard
and his monks, and asked to become members of the
order; numberless towns sent to request St. Bernard
would found a colony within their walls; Emperors,
Kings, and Bishops were equally anxious to be
guided by his advice.

George.   What had made him so well known,
Grandmamma?

Grandmamma.   He had written many very excellent as well as very clever books, my dear little boy,
and this, with the holy, useful and innocent lives of
the monks of Clairvaux, made St. Bernard's a very

prominent position, though still quite a young man.

George. A *what* position? another of your long words, my naughty little Grandmother; tell me what that means.

Grandmother. A prominent position, my child, is that which places a person very much before the eyes of the world; such, for instance, as our good Queen's; such was the great Duke of Wellington's; and many others, who in different ways have been followed by the admiration and esteem of millions of their fellow creatures.

Elizabeth. I am afraid that would make me very vain.

Grandmamma. Not if you were blessed with their good sense. Vanity, I think Dr. Johnson says, is the prevailing weakness of a weak mind; pride the weak point of a strong one.

But to return to our Saint; in the year 1123, he went to pay a visit to the Abbot of the Grande Chartreuse, where Hugh, Bishop of the diocese, received him as a messenger from heaven.

St. Bernard, accompanied by several monks, climbed the rocks, and wild mountains, on the top of which the Carthusians had placed their cells. His visit gave such pleasure to the Solitaries, that its expression is still mentioned in history, though hundreds of years have passed away since it took place, and visitor and visited have all mingled in their parent dust. An anecdote of this visit must certainly amuse you.

George. Tell it to us, dear Grandmamma.

Grandmamma. St. Bernard arrived on a magnificent horse, with a very splendid saddle and bridle; the Prior of the Carthusians was much surprised to see that a monk, professing poverty, should have anything so handsome in his possession. He spoke

on the subject to one of St. Bernard's companions,
and at last it became known to St. Bernard himself,
who smilingly asked to be allowed to see the horse
he had ridden ; he then confessed he had never
noticed the animal or its saddle and bridle; it had
been lent to him at Cluny to ride to the Chartreuse,
and occupied with his meditations he had never
looked at it.

On his return to Clairvaux, a terrible famine
desolated Burgundy: but the valley which years
before he had found an unhealthy swamp was now,
thanks to the labour of the monks, a very granary
of plenty to all Burgundy.

One day he was going to visit the Comte de
Champagne, and he met a procession, leading a very
wicked man, to be put to death. St. Bernard sprang
from his horse, threw himself among the crowd,
and seizing the rope which bound the criminal,—
" trust this man to me," exclaimed St. Bernard, "I
wish to hang him with my own hands."

No one ventured to refuse the excellent Abbot of
Clairvaux, who led the trembling malefactor into
the presence of his Seigneur, the Count of Champagne.

The moment the Count saw the Abbot with the
criminal, he knew that St. Bernard wished to save
his life.

" Reverend Father," said the Count, " what do
you wish? this is a wretch who has deserved Hell a
thousand times already. Would you save a devil?"

Bernard gently replied:

" No, Prince, I do not ask that he should go un-
punished; you were about to make him expiate his
wicked life, by death. Give him to me, I will make
his punishment last as long as his life; he shall
endure the torment of the cross, to the end of his

days; give him to me, I will answer for him to society."

The Prince remained silent.

St. Bernard then took off his own tunic, and put it on the trembling wretch, and with words of gentleness he brought him to Clairvaux, where the wolf was changed into a lamb; he was called Constantine, and well deserved the name, for he persevered in his good life for more than thirty years, and died at Clairvaux, in a most edifying manner.

CHAPTER III.

George. Dear Granny, your children have been making terrible blunders. We did not like the shape of the beds in our own little flower garden, so we determined to cut out some new ones, as a surprise for you, and alas! we cannot make them straight or even; they look what the gardener calls " tipsy," all tumbling on one side. Will you come and help us, best of Grandmothers?

Grandmamma. I can help you without moving from my chair, my wild Grandson, which will be an advantage to both parties. Ask Milsome to give you some old numbers of " the Times," and bring a pair of large scissors. What is to be the shape of the new beds?

George. We thought stars and circles very common, so we wished to have something no one else had got.

Grandmamma. Indeed, my ambitious little man; and pray what may the creation of your taste resemble?

George. A bed like a large capital S —another like a capital B—and the third like a capital C.

Grandmamma. Which means St. Bernard, Clairvaux. Well, my darling, I hope you will print his example on your heart, as well as his name on the turf of your garden; the way to make the bed even, is to sketch it on the paper the size you require, taking care to make an exact pattern; then cut it out, lay it on the turf, follow the outside edge with your knife, and raise the turf with your spade —it must be right, if well sketched.

George. Now, if you are a dear good little Grandmamma, you will sit under the trees, and cut out the pattern: then you can continue telling us the history of St. Bernard, while we are working at our garden.

Grandmamma. I am lucky in having *two* Grandchildren, and luckly in *not* having any more; for I should certainly be wanted in six places at once; however, you must carry out a stool for my feet; and pick up all the snips of paper I shall drop on the grass, in cutting the pattern—now let us go.

Elizabeth. How good of you, dearest Grandmamma, to come out to us; we shall work twice as well.

George. Yes! and she will tell us the story, out here. will not that be nice, Sissy?

Grandmamma. Where did we leave St. Bernard?

Elizabeth. He had just saved poor Constantine's life.

Grandmamma. St. Bernard now devoted himself to a task which he continued all his life, and that was correcting many abuses which had crept into the church.

George. What does that mean?

Grandmamma. It means, my child, that in every

thing in this world, evil becomes mixed up with good; the greatest number of sins in society are produced by people who try to acquire either money, or power, for themselves by unjust means. Thus for instance, Emperors and Kings had the power of appointing Bishops, and Ecclesiastics to high dignities, subject to the approval of the Pope. If the Sovereign was an unprincipled person, he sold the bishopric to some unsuitable man, and the Pope being at a distance and trusting to the Sovereign's better means of judging, gave his consent to the nomination. Here then we will suppose is a bad man, placed in a position for which he had not the necessary virtues; he wants money, bad people invariably do, (and good ones too very often); but among the numerous clergy under his orders there are many very excellent pious men, full of information, and that Christian humility which like charity " seeketh not itself;" but they are not rich, for all they possess is shared with the poor.

A good benefice becomes vacant, the worldly man who has been made Bishop, wishes to sell this living quietly, to who ever will give the most for it. The good members of the clergy first would not agree to such a mode of advancement, and secondly they have not the means even if they had the inclination. Perhaps one of the king's courtiers hears of it; he has a wild, or a lazy idle son, for whom he knows not how to provide; he buys the benefice, on condition that the Bishop will give the ordination necessary to enable him to receive the emoluments belonging to his new position; now, there is a second unfit person put into the church by unfair means; and willing to admit others, in the same manner he himself entered. The same sort of thing went on among the monks, particularly in the order of Cluny, only they could

not sell their dignities, like the seculars; however
this order, once so saintly, so fervent, had become
wealthy; and as their riches increased, their humble
Christian virtues were sadly neglected. Their Abbot,
Peter the Venerable, was an admirable man, who
lamented the relaxed state of their order, and was
the personal friend of St. Bernard, who now determined, as I have before told you, to devote himself
to bringing back the ancient beautiful discipline of
the Christian Church.

Elizabeth. Did not the monks of Cluny dislike
St. Bernard?

Grandmamma. Of course they did my love; but
among their number were numerous excellent men,
who rejoiced, that their luxurious life was to be
altered. St. Bernard published his celebrated letter
called his " Apology," in which he enters into the
details of their interior arrangement, which he considered unfit for men who had left the world to
mortify their flesh; he complains of them drinking
wine without water, and having two courses of fish
on fast days.

George. Did he order them beech leaves?

Grandmamma. He had no power to alter. only
to expose, and he did it so thoroughly, that a general
assembly of the Abbots of Cluny was held, to take
counsel together on the means of remedying existing
evils.

In 1124 St. Bernard's sister, Hombeline, who
had been living in the world ever since her
marriage, arrived at Clairvaux to see her brother,
who left her at Fontaines years before, when she
was a little girl, and he and all the brothers were
asking their poor old father's blessing, previous to
going to Citeaux. Hombeline in a splendid carriage,
stopped at the gate of the monastery, and asked to

speak to the Abbot; but St. Bernard disliking the luxury which she displayed could not make up his mind to see her, and her other brothers refused likewise; poor Hombeline, cut to the heart, burst into tears.

" I know that I am a sinner," cried she—" I know that I am a great sinner; but did not our Saviour die for such persons as I am?—If my brother despises my body, let not the servant of Almighty God despise my soul."

At these affecting words the gates of the monastery opened, and Bernard and his brothers came forth to comfort their sister in her sorrow.

St. Bernard talked seriously to her, about the worldly life she was leading, and for the guide of her future existence, he recommended her to follow the admirable example of their mother. Bernard worked upon her feelings and on her affection for their exemplary parent, so much that Hombeline returned to her princely home, with a changed heart, and after the death of her husband, she took the religious habit and died a pious excellent Christian.

Elizabeth. I never heard of such a family; they all leave the world to become monks or nuns, with as much ease and composure as if it was an act of no importance.

Grandmamma. It has always been regarded as something inexplicable; much of course is to be attributed to the example of their mother, whose wish as a girl was to be a Religious; her early lessons all tended to teach them detachment from the trammels of this life, and then the extraordinary goodness and wisdom of their brother finished the work their parent had commenced. St. Bernard, who had done so much good by exposing the laxity of other orders of monks, especially that of Cluny, was very strict

in keeping up the piety and discipline of Clairvaux,
and a story is told that shews curiously enough the
manner in which he succeeded.

George. A story—I am so glad—I love a story,
Grandmamma.

Grandmamma. I know you do my own boy, and
I am glad too, when I can remember one in the life
of Bernard, which I think will amuse you. A poor
lay brother of Clairvaux, had learned to be meek
and humble of heart; all the monks said he had
never been seen out of temper, or impatient, and if
any one accused him, whether justly or unjustly, he
immediately said a prayer for them.

One day being sent on some business, he was
obliged to pass alone through a thick forest, and
when he was least thinking of it, robbers attacked
him, took away his horse, and all his clothes, and
then left him to get home as he could. No sooner
were they gone than the poor monk threw himself
on the grass, and prayed to God aloud to forgive
them for what they had done; they perhaps had
never been taught how wrong it was; and he continued for some time begging forgiveness for those
who had so cruelly used him. One of them was
not far off, and hearing the monk's voice, he crept
back to see to whom he was talking; but not per-
ceiving any other person, he listened to what the
poor man was saying, and when he had heard him
praying for the band who had robbed him, the ban-
dit ran to his companions, and exclaimed, "Woe to
us, miserable wretches, he is a saintly man; one of
those good monks of Clairvaux."

They all went quietly to look at and listen to him,
for he was still praying; and the contrast between
his goodness, and their life of sin struck them so
much, that they brought his clothes and his horse

back to him, at the same time asking forgiveness for what they had done.

George. I think, Grandmamma, that people were better in those days than they are now. I am afraid if any very good holy man was robbed by a gang of thieves in London, they would not return his clothes because he prayed God to forgive them.

Elizabeth. I agree with George.

Grandmamma. There is law, and justice for poor as well as rich in our nineteenth century, a thing unknown in the twelfth; but whether crime is more rife now, would take some time to consider; crimes are different as society alters. Men such as Paul, Strahan and Bates were unknown; men like Palmer were frequently encountered; but luckily those subtle poisons used in after times by Ruggiero, and some of the Borgias, are now totally lost.

George. Where have we left St. Bernard, Grandmamma?

Grandmamma. I regret to say, that he is very ill at Clairvaux, and obliged to leave the convent and live once more in the little hut, where he sent for his old friend, William de St. Thierry, to come and stay with him. William was ill at Rheims, but left his bed to obey Bernard's wishes, looking forward with delight to the idea of being ill together in the hut. William wrote down their conversations every evening, for fear that the words of so good a man as Bernard might be forgotten. "When Septuagesima Sunday was approaching," said William, "I felt well enough to leave my bed and walk about, so I began to prepare for returning home; but Bernard forbade my doing so until Quinquagesima. I submitted, for my weakness seemed to render it necessary; until that moment I had eaten meat by his order, but now I thought I might leave it off.

3

Bernard desired me not to abstain, but thinking myself well enough to go without animal food, I quietly declined taking any without mentioning it to him.   My illness returned with redoubled violence; so great was the agony I endured, I thought I could not live through the night, and early the next morning I sent for the saint, who approached my bed with a stern countenance, instead of the gentle smile with which he was wont to greet me.

"'Well,' said he, 'what do you mean to eat to-day?'

"'Whatever you order,' I replied.

"'Well, be at ease, you will not die.'

"The pain left me, and my strength gradually returning, I was able to leave Clairvaux in a few days, with the good man's blessing."

Elizabeth. Only fancy, Grandmamma, two noblemen of the present day, looking forward with pleasure to being ill together in a little hut, just large enough to contain two small beds, and two chairs, a clay floor, and no fire-place. Imagine the Archbishop of Canterbury sending such an invitation to some great dignitary of the church of England, and its being accepted as a favour.

Grandmamma. Yes, my child, it seems ridiculous to our pampered ideas of modern luxury and refinement; but we may take a much higher model of perfection, one to whom Bernard, excellent as he was, cannot bear even the shadow of comparison. Look at the head and founder of our Church, our blessed Lord, who lived for many years in a little cottage at Nazareth, in all the hourly privations of poverty; probably assisting St. Joseph in his trade as a carpenter; and aiding His blessed Mother in the different labours which peasants are necessarily obliged to perform. The well where she went daily for water, is still shewn to the traveller, and over the cottage a church has been built.

Elizabeth. If people reflected upon that, would it not cure them of being proud?

Grandmamma. It would certainly go a good way towards it; but we live, as though we did not think it incumbent upon us, to strive to imitate our Lord's example, nor even the many specimens of Christian perfection, which are so numerous in the early ages of the Church.

That however was not St. Bernard's way, he forgot himself, in his constant endeavours to assist his fellow creatures, and we shall now find him engaged in a new plan, which will, I am sure, delight you, George.

George. I am very glad of it, dear Granny; for I hope you will not be angry, when I say, I have found his history not *quite quite* so amusing as it was at first.

Grandmamma. Well my boy, he will redeem himself in your opinion, for he is now going to make soldiers.

George. St. Bernard!—impossible—he would not be a soldier himself; he would not allow his brothers to remain in the army, and now he changes in this extraordinary manner,—what can it mean, Grandmamma? I am as curious, as——a girl—I beg your pardon, Miss Elizabeth.

Elizabeth. Granted, master George; but if you are as curious as a girl, by which I suppose you mean a young lady, it is a pity you are not as *civil* as they are likewise.

George. A truce! a truce! Sister mine, I am dying to hear about St. Bernard's soldiers—what could they be like, Grandmamma?

Grandmamma. In the commencement of the

twelfth century, Jerusalem was conquered by the
Saracens; and religious zeal inflamed the greater
part of the Christian knights, to fight for the deliverance of the Holy Sepulchre. Several French
knights, of the company of Godefroi de Bouillon,
had associated themselves together, about the year
1118, and obtained from the King of Jerusalem, a
dwelling on the site of the ancient Temple of Solomon; hence, they took their name as Knights of the
Temple, or Templars, (Milites Templi).

Elizabeth. What are those two last words, Grandmamma?

George. Latin, not meant for young ladies—too
difficult.

Elizabeth. But I should like to know, notwith-
standing—if you will translate them, dear Grandmamma; for I see that poor little George cannot.

George. Miss Impertinence! they mean Soldiers
of the Temple.

Grandmamma. Well, that difficulty being settled
to our satisfaction, we will continue their history.
They lived together like monks, but subject to
military, as well as religious discipline, under the
command of Hughes de Payen—their first Grand-
master. Their war cry was a verse of the Psalms,
" non nobis Domine, non nobis, sed nomini, tuo da
gloriam."

Elizabeth. Poor little George; more Latin, translate it if you please.

George. (Looking very red;) " Not to us, O Lord,
not to us, to thy name be the glory."

Grandmamma. Very well, my dear boy; it gives
me the greatest pleasure to see that you have pro-
fited so much by your Latin lessons. To return to
our Templars; about the year 1128, they came to
Rome, to ask the Pope for a rule of life. Honorius

foresaw the advantage of such an order, and sent Hughes de Payen and his brethren to Troyes, where the French Bishops were then met in conclave, charging them to examine the proposed plan of the order, and give it a definite form. St. Bernard was selected to draw up the statutes, which, as might be expected from his character, combined religious fervour with military ardour. "Go," said the holy Abbot to the Templars, "go good knights, pursue with an intrepid heart, the enemies of the cross of our Saviour, well assured that neither death, nor life, will be able to separate you from the love of God, which is in Jesus Christ. In all perils, and on all occasions repeat these words of the Apostle, Living or dead we are God's; conquerors or martyrs rejoice, you are the Lord's."

After the council of Troyes, St. Bernard, at his earnest request, was allowed to return to his cloister, where he spent eighteen months in carrying the monastery to the highest point of perfection, and found his feeble health renewed and strengthened, in the peaceable exercise of a religious life.

CHAPTER IV.

George. Best of Grandmothers, the tiresome lessons are over; the Governess is pretending to read, but I suspect she is fast asleep, and if she did not awake for a hundred years, like the sleeping Beauty in the wood, I should not be very sorry, at least I am not the knight who would fly to her rescue; and better than all, Sissy and I have carried your chair under the trees, close to our own little garden, where we are going to work, and your spectacles and your knitting are all waiting.

Grandmamma. I do not think that you speak very respectfully of your Governess; my child, you ought to try to love her; think of the trouble she takes every day with you and Elizabeth, does not that deserve some gratitude and affection ?

George. Indeed, Granny, you have taken such a big piece of my heart for yourself, that all which remains Sissy has got, and not one corner can I find to put Miss Thomas into.

Elizabeth. Ha! Ha!—Grandmamma, what will you say to George's reason?

Grandmamma. That I fear you are both sadly spoiled children: and now let us talk of St. Bernard, instead of poor Miss Thomas; but what are you looking at so attentively Elizabeth?

Elizabeth. In turning up a piece of turf, for our new bed, I found this large grey insect, covered over with numbers of ants; it seems almost dead.

Grandmamma. It is called the Grey Puceron; the ants are fond of sucking it to death. The Puceron lives on the roots of the grass, and would prove most destructive, if not destroyed by its enemies; so true it is, my children, that all living creatures devour each other for food ; we eat a various number of animals, and *en revanche* one small worm makes its revolting meal of our decaying bodies; a fact which would cure us of pride, if we reflected on the humiliating lesson it inculcates. But humility reminds us of your favourite St. Bernard ; I conclude that you decoyed me here, that I might continue telling you his history, while you both work at your new garden.

Elizabeth. Yes, Grandmamma, that was our plan.

Grandmamma. The next period of his life will

hardly be so interesting as the last, for it contains what may be called his political history, and therefore I shall condense it as much as possible.

At this time the church was torn in pieces by internal dissension, on account of two rival candidates seizing on the Tiara ; Innocent the Second and Anacletus the Second ; St. Bernard espoused the cause of the former; thinking conscientiously that he was the proper person to be the head of the Church; and against his wish and will, our great hero was once more sent from his convent, to Italy, to soothe the broils that have ever been the bane and misery of that beautiful Peninsula. While residing at Milan, the inhabitants and the clergy implored him to accept the Archiepiscopal throne of their city; but such was his dread of worldly titles, worldly riches, and all the dangers they entail, that he used every effort to escape the snare. In the year 1135, he received permission to go back to his beloved Clairvaux. He returned home through Switzerland, where the shepherds descended from the mountains to ask his blessing.

Most historians attribute the name of the two celebrated mountains of the Valais, to the enthusiastic reverence the Swiss felt for his many shining virtues; but other historians mention that Bernard de Menthon, archdeacon of Aoste, overthew an idol of Jupiter, which had been placed on the mountain, and in its stead built a monastery which was to be an asylum for travellers. This is the celebrated place where so many thousand of our countrymen enjoy every year the hospitable care of the good sons of St. Bernard.

George. That is where those clever dogs are kept, is it not Grandmamma? how I should like to have one, it should never leave me night or day.

Grandmamma. They certainly are wonderfully sagacious, but I am sorry to say, that when they leave the care of the good monks, they also say adieu to much of their praiseworthy behaviour; I have known several persons who having brought them to England, were obliged to have them shot, from their incorrigible propensity for mutton; they constantly get out at night, and having once commenced this habit of sheep-killing, nothing can conquer its inveteracy.

To return to our great man; when he arrived at Langres, he found his monks, who had come to meet him at the news of his approach. "All," says his biographer, "threw themselves on their knees, and asked his blessing; each embraced their revered Father, and full of joy conducted him to Clairvaux." As soon as he crossed the threshold of his beloved home, he went to return thanks in the church; and assembling his children in the chapter-room, he made them a tender and affectionate exhortation, while they listened with delight to the soft tones of a voice which they never heard excepting to use kind and gentle words.

Clairvaux was much too small for the ever increasing number of men of all ranks of life, who asked to be admitted into the fold of which St. Bernard was the shepherd: he disliked the expense of pulling down a building which a few years before it had given them so much trouble to build; "what will people think of us," said he to the monks, "if we now destroy what we have so lately made; besides, we have no money?"

The monks replied :—

"You must either reject those whom God has sent you, or you must build rooms to lodge them in;

woe to us, if for the fear of expense, we should put
a stop to the development of any work of God."

These representations decided the Abbot; when it
was known in France, that Clairvaux must be re-
built for want of room, assistance was sent from all
quarters, for the fame of St. Bernard was the glory
of all Christendom, and every one knew that he
never did anything without good reasons.

A hundred new novices quickly filled the ad-
ditional cells, and the blessing of heaven seemed to
descend upon every work that his good and pious
servant undertook.

About this time a monk of Clairvaux fell ill in
Normandy, and the Abbot, full of care for the comfort
of his children, wished to have him sent for, that he
might at least have the consolation of dying at
home; Guido, the elder brother of the Abbot, who
managed the affairs of the monastery, feared the
expense of such a long journey, and spoke of it to
St. Bernard.

"What!" exclaimed the good Abbot, in accents
of surprise, "do you think more of the horses and
the money than of one of your brothers? since you
will not have him rest among us, depend upon it
you will not lie here yourself."

The prediction was soon verified, for Guido went
to Pontigny on business, and after a short illness
died, and was buried there.

St. Bernard's affliction was very great, for he tenderly loved his brother, but he did not allow his
grief to interfere with the numberless duties that
devolved on the head of such an immense establish-
ment, a lesson we should all do well to remember.

But St. Bernard was not long permitted to remain
quiet in his beloved monastery; troubles again broke
out in Italy, and in 1137 he was ordered to return

thither, which he did immediately, taking his brother
Gerard to be the companion of his long and dangerous journey.

George. I think he was a very unlucky man in
some ways, for he left the world because he hated
its bustle and wickedness, and retired to a swamp
in the middle of forests, that he might be quiet, and
as he said, "study the ways of God, among the
beeches and oaks;" and it appears to me that he is
scarcely ever allowed to remain there, but is always
sent into the middle of quarrels, contentions, and
battles, to try to make every one as good as himself.

Grandmamma. Rather a Herculean task, even for
our great hero.

Elizabeth. Can you call such a man a hero? I
thought it was applicable to people of the world, not
to those who had left it for God.

Grandmamma. They are the soldiers of the Almighty; they fight and devote their lives to His
service, in the same way that our great men, such
as Wellington and Nelson, spent their days in add-
ing to the glory of their earthly sovereign; there is
this material difference, the gallant soldiers of our
English Monarch receive in this world the honours
and distinctions they so well deserve, while the
soldier of the Cross trusts entirely to those words
of the Gospel, which promise rewards in heaven to
those who leave houses and riches for God's sake.
They cannot accept anything from the world they
have left, and they wait humbly and patiently until
it pleases their Almighty Chief to call them to their
recompense, "Where the wicked cease from trou-
bling, and the weary are at rest."

Elizabeth. Then at this rate every missionary
who leaves England or France to teach Christianity

to the idolators, like Abbe Huc, or Dr. Livingstone, is entitled to be called a hero?

Grandmamma. I think so, my dear; and what is far beyond it, many earn the glorious palm of martyrdom.

We have left our Saint at Viterbo, where his brother Gerard became very ill, and nothing the doctors could devise was of any avail, and Gerard resigned himself to God's will, and prepared for death. St. Bernard entreated and conjured the Almighty to spare his brother, at least till his return to Clairvaux, and the cry of the faithful servant was heard by that ear which is ever open to our necessities and petitions: Gerard recovered, and they continued their journey towards Rome, where the Emperor Lothaiius and the Pope awaited their arrival. St. Bernard succeeded once more in putting an end to strife and bloodshed, which had recommenced between the partisans of the rival Popes, for at the death of Anacletus the Cardinals who were in his interest elected Cardinal Gregory, who took the name of Victor. By the power of St. Bernard's prayers, and the sweetness of his eloquence, Victor became touched by the sad scenes of anarchy to which the maintenance of his supposed rights would give rise, and a few days after his election he came by night to St. Bernard, with all the appearance of a sincere repentance. St. Bernard received him with exceeding joy, and led him to the feet of the real Pope, Innocent the Second, against whom neither arms, schism, wickedness, nor any effort of sinful man, had been able to prevail.

Thus once more, by the untiring efforts of our good Saint, was peace restored, and the gratitude of the Romans was so great, that whenever he appeared in the streets nobles formed his train, the people shouted " *Vivas*," the ladies knelt for his blessing, and all crowded around him with the liveliest testimonies of respect.

Five days after the restoration of peace he sought and received a reluctant permission to retire once more from the unceasing broils of the world, to the peaceful life of his beloved Clairvaux, where he arrived at the end of the year 1138.

At the urgent request of the grateful Pope St. Bernard sent a little colony of his children to Rome, headed by Bernard of Pisa, who subsequently was called to the Tiara, under the name of Eugenius the Third.

Scarcely had St. Bernard returned to his monastery, when his brother Gerard became very ill. He immediately recollected the prayer he had offered up to God at Viterbo, " Spare him, O Lord, only until his return to Clairvaux." When Bernard's malady commenced, they both recollected the limitation of the petition, and both felt that the bitter hour of parting had arrived, and poor Gerard drew his last breath as he finished chanting the verse of a Psalm, a circumstance which reminds us forcibly of the death of the kind good Mother they had so fondly loved, and whose blameless life they had ever wished to imitate.

We shall now see St. Bernard under a new aspect; like David, he had given way to grief while his brother was lying between life and death, but the moment suspense was over, and the lifeless body of Gerard lay before him, Bernard stifled every groan, swallowed every tear, and seemed turned to stone.

He arranged all the sorrowful preparations for the funeral; he chanted the Office for the Dead. Never before had one of his spiritual children died without his shedding many tears, and the difference was the more remarkable, that the monks who loved Gerard sincerely, were almost all weeping. " How can it be," said the religious among themselves, " that he commands himself so well?"

George. I do not think it at all to be admired, Grandmamma. I have a terrible suspicion that it was want of feeling. I wished he had cried like the others, I should have liked him so much better.

Elizabeth. Perhaps he had so schooled his every weakness, that at last he learned to look upon feeling as one of them, and killed it with the rest.

Grandmamma. Stay, my children, do not judge so hastily. Let us hear his own explanation of the strange fact.

On the very day of the funeral he ascended the pulpit to explain the Canticles, as was his habit; but he suddenly stopped, his voice was choked, tears deluged his face, and he leaned his head on the front of the pulpit, struggling with the sobs that heaved his bosom. I will read his own words to you, they are the best proof whether or not he felt his bereavement.

" My affliction, and the grief which overwhelms me, compel me to break off this discourse. Why should I dissemble what I feel? The fire which I conceal consumes and devours me; the more I strive to keep it in, the more does its violence increase; how then can I explain to you Solomon's song of gladness, while my soul is so very sad and heavy? . . . . Hitherto I have striven, I have been able to master myself, fearing lest the sentiments of nature should overpower those of faith; I followed the sad procession without shedding a tear, while all around me wept abundantly. I stood with dry eyes beside that grave, the sight whereof wrung my heart.

" In my priestly vestments I said the prayers of the Church over the deceased; I cast with my own hands, as the custom is, earth on the loved body, which will so soon be reduced to similar dust.

" You marvelled that I melted not into tears, you who wept less for the deceased than for me. What heart indeed, were, it of bronze, but must be touched to see me survive Gerard. But I cannot command my feelings. . . . . . Let them appear, then, before the eyes of my children, that they may have compassion on me, and the more abundantly and tenderly console me.

" You know, my children, what deep cause I have for sorrow, for you knew the faithful companion who has now left me alone in the path wherein we walked together; you knew the services he rendered me; the care he took of all things; the diligence with which he performed his actions; the sweetness which characterized all his conduct. Who can be to me what he was? Who ever loved me as he did? He was my brother by the ties of blood; but he was far more my brother by the ties of grace, and the strong bond of religion. Pity my lot, you who know all this. I was weak in body, and he supported me; I was timid, and he encouraged me; I was slow, and he excited me to action; I was wanting in memory and foresight, and he perpetually reminded me of my duties. Oh! my brother, wherefore hast thou been 'torn from me? Oh ! my well-beloved! why didst thou leave thy poor brother ? Oh! man according to mine own heart, why has death parted us, who were bound so closely together during life?

" Death alone could have made this cruel separa-

tion. Death, implacable death, the enemy of all
sweet things, could alone have broken this link of
love, so gentle, so tender, so lively, so intense!

"Cruel death, by taking away one, thou hast
killed two at once; for the life which remains to me
is heavier than death.

"Yes, my Gerard, it would have been better for
me to die than to lose thee.

"Thy zeal animated me in all my duties.

"Thy fidelity was my comfort at all times.

"Thy prudence accompanied all my steps.

"We rejoiced together in our union; our mutual
converse was dear to us both, but I alone have lost
this happiness, for thou hast found far greater con-
solations; thou dost enjoy the mutual presence of
Jesus Christ, and the company of angels; but what
have I to fill the void which I have left?

"Ah! what would I give to know what are thy
feelings now, towards the brother who was thine
only beloved? If now that thou art plunged in
the floods of divine light, thou art still permitted to
think of our miseries, to concern thyself about our
sorrows,—for perhaps though thou hast known us
according to the flesh, thou wilt know us no more.
He who is attached to God, is but one spirit with
God.

"Now, 'God is love,' and the more truly a soul
is united with God, the fuller it is of love.

"God is impassible, not insensible; for the quali-
ties most proper to Him are compassion and forgiveness, therefore thou needest be merciful, who art
united to the source of mercy; and although thou
art delivered from misery, thou wilt not cease to
compassionate our sufferings.

"Thou hast laid aside thine infirmities but not

thy charity, for 'charity abideth,' says the apostle.
Ah! no, thou wilt not forget us through eternity.

"Alas! whom shall I now consult in my sorrows;
to whom shall I have recourse in my difficulties?
Who will bear with me the burthen of my woes;
who will defend me from the perils which surround
me?

"It was the eye of Gerard which guided my
steps.

"Thy heart, oh, my brother, was more laden
than mine with the cares which overwhelm me.
With thy words of sweetness thou wouldst fill my
place, and set me free from secular conversations to
enjoy the silence which I love. He stayed the flood
of visits, and would not suffer all persons to come
to me, without distinction, and absorb my leisure.
He took upon himself to receive them, and brought
me only such as he judged it fitting I should see.

"It was not that his taste led him to these trouble-
some offices, but he undertook them to spare me,
and to assist me, believing my repose to be more
advantageous to the monastery than his own; and
assuredly I could repose in all security while he was
acting as the light of my eyes, my heart, my tongue.

"Thy hand was indefatigable, oh my brother,
thine eye single, thy heart pure, according as it
is written:

"'The just man meditates wisdom, and his tongue
speaks prudently.'

"I was called Abbot of Clairvaux, but he fulfilled
the painful functions of my charge, and thus by
self-devotion, he gained for me the necessary time
for my exercises, my prayers, and my studies. my
preaching, and my interior practices. I mourn, but
I murmur not. One has been justly punished, the
other deservedly crowned. As we were in truth,

but one in heart, the sword of death pierced both at
once, and cut us in two parts, one is in Heaven, the
other in the dust of this world.

" Some may perhaps say, 'your grief is carnal.'
I deny not that it is human, as I deny not that I
am a man. Nay, more, I deny not that it is carnal,
since I myself am carnal, the slave of sin, subject
to misery, destined to die. Could Gerard be taken
from me, my brother in blood, my son in religion,
my father in his care of me, my only beloved in his
affection, my very soul in his love; he is taken
from me, and must not I feel it? God grant, my
Gerard, that I may not have lost thee, but that thou
mayest only precede me, and that I may follow thee
whither thou art gone.

" You, my brethren, called me to witness a miracle, a man rejoicing in his death ; 'oh! death, where
was thy victory,—oh! grave, where was thy sting?'
To him thou art no sting, but a song of jubilee;
and death, that mother of sorrows, a source of joy.
I had no sooner reached the bedside of the dying
man, than I heard him pronounce aloud the words
of our Lord, ' Father, into thy hands I commend
my spirit.' Then repeating that same verse, and
dwelling on the words, ' Father! Father!' he
turned towards me, and said with a smile :

" ' Oh! what goodness in God to be the Father of
men, and what glory for men to be the children of
God!'

" Thus died he whom we all deplore, and I con-
fess that it almost changed my affliction into rejoicing, so much did his evident happiness make me
forget my misery."

George. Grandmamma, is that all?

Grandmamma. No, my love, it is not all, neither
have I read it verbatim, but merely selected here

4

and there the passages which I thought most likely to catch your attention.

Elizabeth. (Crying). It is so sad, so beautiful, so melancholy, I cannot help crying, dear Grandmamma, though I know it is very foolish.

Grandmamma. No, my child, it is not foolish; people cry at an opera—at a play—even at a silly novel—and why should we be ashamed of shedding tears at the recital of a scene so touching and so true?

George. I will never say that St. Bernard had no feeling again.

Grandmamma. I think I have seldom read any description where the woeful workings of the heart are rendered more apparent to the reader, and no one can study the pious gentle heart of St. Bernard without feeling benefited by the Christian sentiments it reveals.

CHAPTER V.

Not long after the death of Gerard, St. Bernard received a visit from St. Malachi, Metropolitan of Ireland, who was attracted to Clairvaux by the world-wide reputation of its holy Abbot. Malachi was on his road to Rome, on the business of the diocese, but he was so edified by the pious and truly Christian life, led by the good monks, that he asked to give up the dignities of his position, and enrol himself among the children of St. Bernard. This the Abbot would not permit, but on St. Malachi's return from Rome, on a subsequent journey, he again went to Clairvaux, and there, according to his

own desire and prediction, he died in the arms of
St. Bernard, and was buried in the church of the
monastery.

In the year 1145, Bernard of Pisa, who headed
the little colony of monks, whom St. Bernard sent
to form a monastery of the order in Rome, was
suddenly informed that he had been elected to fill
the vacant throne in the Vatican. Pope Lucius was
dead. Bernard of Pisa was one of the most nervous
of the brethren. His occupation at Clairvaux was
to tend the stove and make a fire for the monks,
who were benumbed with cold after matins, because
of the scantiness of their clothing. Even this mis-
sion seemed beyond his powers.

George. He was not likely to make a very good
Pope,—what a pity to have chosen him, Grandmamma.

Grandmamma. A most extraordinary change
came over him, after he had received consecration,
he was equal to his situation, and seemed to have
discarded all his previous nervousness. He took
the name of Eugenius the Third, and for him St. Bernard wrote " the Book of the Consideration," which
has been the Manual of all succeeding pontiffs.

George. Dear Grandmamma, will you be so very
kind as to skip all about his writings, and give us
some more stories, they amuse me the most, and I
recollect them best?

Grandmamma. Yes, dear boy, luckily history
furnishes me with what you call " a story," and one
after your own heart, about a fight, such a fight as
made the world shake, while it looked on in trembling anxiety.

George. Oh ! delightful—what glorious fun !
I do so love to hear about a battle,—now Sissy,
listen !

Grandmamma. You remember Godefroi de Bouillon, who fought for the deliverance of the Holy
Sepulchre ?

Elizabeth. Oh! yes, quite well. A noble French
knight.

Grandmamma. His brother Baldwin founded a
principality in Mesopotamia, of which Edessa was
the capital. It was taken, after a horrible massacre,
by the Sultan of Bagdad, in 1144. This made
Antioch tremble, and Jerusalem, governed by Melis-
sinda, widow of Fulk of Anjou, regent during the
minority of her son Baldwin the Third. At this
time a cry of distress arose from the East, which
resounded through Western Christendom. The
misfortunes of the Holy Land excited universal
sorrow, especially in France. The new kingdom
had been founded by the arms of France, French
princes were its possessors. A Frenchman was seated
on the throne of Jerusalem, and though every
Christian state was interested in the preservation of
Jerusalem, first on account of its sanctity, and
secondly on account of the safety of the numerous
pilgrims who flocked from all Christian countries
to the birth-place of their faith; still, France, ever
in the front rank, where glory is to be won, whether
under Louis VII., or Napoleon III.—France considered her national honour more at stake than that
of any other country, because French princes were
the rulers of the Holy Land.

The news of the capture of Edessa reached Paris
in 1145, and was followed by a letter from our old
acquaintance who used to light the stove at Clairvaux, now Pope Eugenius Third. This letter was
addressed not only to the King, but to the French
people. Louis held his court at Bourges, where he
summoned the Bishops and nobles of his kingdom,

and confided to them his intention of leading another crusade; but many were the difficulties to surmount. The old knights remembered the terrible hardships that the gallant Godefroi de Bouillon had to encounter—they knew the obstacles to be overcome, want of water, want of roads, want of proper means of transport for ammunition and food.

Suger, the prudent minister of Louis VII., thought of the immense expense of such an undertaking, and of the drained state of the royal coffers; but Louis, firm in his determination, knew that there was but one man in France who could overcome all these contending opinions, provided he considered the undertaking just, and for God's greater honour. Can you guess to whom King Louis determined to trust the decision, whether or no the second crusade should take place?

George. Why, of course, he asked St. Bernard.

Grandmamma. Again our great recluse was taken from the peaceful monastery he loved so well, and summoned to the assembly at Vezelai, to be the umpire of conflicting interests and opinions. Little did the minister Suger imagine that he would warmly embrace the idea of a new crusade, and renew by his thrilling eloquence, the wonders of the age of Peter the Hermit.

The Abbot of Clairvaux was in his 54 year, when the orders of the Pope once more sent him from the monastery where he had remained for three years in the repose his failing health so much required, but his fragile frame was so weakened by austerities and long sufferings, that his life seemed prolonged by a miracle. It was with difficulty he could stand, and an old chronicler says, "he was almost dead, you would have thought he was going to breathe his last." Yet this frail body was animated by superhuman strength, when he became the organ of any undertaking which was for the honour of that Father in heaven, whose name he hallowed, and whose will he did, according to the best of his ability on earth, as he hoped soon to do it in Heaven.

The Pope, knowing his high endowments and supernatural gifts, forgot his bodily infirmities; and Bernard had practised obedience and self-denial too long to allow his sufferings to interfere with any advantage which Christianity might derive from his eloquence: at once, and without a murmur, he undertook the fatiguing burthen of preaching the crusade, which commenced in Holy Week, 1146.

Elizabeth. Why is it, dear Granny, that Christendom no longer produces such men as St. Bernard?

Grandmamma. I conclude, my love, that God no longer requires them,—He knows best: "high as the heavens above the earth, so are his ways above our ways."

The fame of the sacred orator drew immense crowds to Vezelay. Louis Seventh, and his Queen, Eleanor, (who afterwards married our Henry Second,) ascended the platform, from whence St. Bernard was to preach to the multitude of people who had congregated to hear the great man of the age. He had not preached long, when his audience shouted, "The cross, the cross, give us the cross!" Louis Seventh, deeply moved, threw himself at the feet of the holy Abbot, and solemnly pledged himself to march to the assistance of the Holy Land. The Queen, following his example, asked, and received from St. Bernard the pilgrim's cross. The supply of crosses proving quite insufficient, St. Bernard tore his own garments to make crosses of the fragments, and thus, in tattered clothes he remained for hours distributing the sacred sign, that glorious symbol which distinguishes the Christian from the idolator.

George. Grand! that is grand! how I wish I had seen him, in his torn gown. I know I should have asked for it too, and shouted as loud as the rest.

Grandmamma. Probably you would, my child; the idea was a lofty one; its execution was fraught with misfortune to millions.

Elizabeth. Do you not admire the Crusades, Grandmamma? I own I have often regretted that I did not live in those days, that I might have shared its dangers.

Grandmamma. I have the greatest respect for the motive, but I lament the number of human lives so unhappily sacrificed; however, let us return to St. Bernard, who was sent from town to town to preach, in order to enrol soldiers under the standard of the Cross. To his astonishment he received an intimation that, by universal consent, he had been promoted to march at the head of the expedition, in command of the enormous army of Crusaders.

Elizabeth. Why, Grandmamma, he was so ill he could scarcely walk. How could such fatigue and responsibility be imposed on him?

Grandmamma. Bernard refused the honour, and referred his cause to Pope Eugenius, begging him "not to abandon him to the caprice of man." The Pope consented, and Bernard escaped the elevated dignity, so contrary to his taste for quiet recollection and humble usefulness among his brethren at Clairvaux.

His next labour was the defence of the Jews, who had been cruelly persecuted in many parts of Germany; at Cologne especially they were subjected to cruelties that were a disgrace to a Christian nation, and the voice of Bernard, ever ready in the cause of humanity, thundered against men who could so wantonly tarnish the lustre of the religion they professed, but whose spirit they evidently did not understand.

Year 1146. At the request of the Bishop of Constance, he sailed up the Rhine, to preach the Crusade in his large diocese. This voyage was one continued triumph, for at the prayer of St. Bernard it pleased Almighty God to cure many afflicted persons of their infirmities. On his arrival at Constance his clothes were torn off to make crosses, which, he says, "he found very inconvenient," as he was so frequently obliged to accept a new habit.

Our Saint had promised the Emperor Conrad the Third to be present at the Diet of Spires, during the Christmas festival. The inhabitants of the adjacent villages waited on the banks of the river, that they might receive his blessing as the vessel which bore so precious a freight, passed towards its destination.

On his arrival at Spires, the clergy and laity went to meet him in procession, and conducted him to the cathedral, where he was received by the Emperor Conrad, and the Princes of the empire. They advanced from the great door singing hymns, and brass plates were laid down to mark to succeeding ages the footsteps of this most holy and most humble minded disciple of our Blessed Saviour.

St. Bernard was present at the coronation of the Emperor, which took place during the religious ceremonies of the season. But he had great trouble in reconciling the feelings of enmity which many members of the Diet felt towards each other, and he endeavoured in vain to make them forget their

personal animosities, and devote all their energies
to the Crusade. The Emperor was more inclined
towards this great undertaking than the Princes of the
empire, and with less stern determination announced
that he would give his definitive reply on the following day. This was a critical moment. Bernard
would not wait until the next 'day. He was cele-
brating mass in presence of the court, after which
he pronounced a moving discourse on the woes of
the Holy Land, and addressing himself to the
Emperor, he exclaimed: "Oh man, what wilt thou
answer in the day of judgment!" Conrad was
struck to the heart, and replied, with tears, "I am
ready to devote my life to the Lord, and to go
whithersoever He calls me!"

Meanwhile St. Bernard took the sacred banner
from the altar, and placed it in the Emperor's hands;
at the same moment the princes of the empire knelt
at the feet of the holy preacher, and asked for the
pilgrim's cross. This enthusiasm gained all ranks
of the people, and even robbers and brigands came
to do penance, and vowed "they would shed their
blood for Christ's sake."

George. That was a lucky thing, I think, Grandmamma; for as all the soldiers and the good people
were to leave Germany for the Holy Land, the
robbers would have made a good harvest had they
remained behind.

Grandmamma. It shows us clearly, my dear little
boy, the strength of that enthusiasm which could
make even robbers prefer the risks and hardships of
the Crusade to the golden opportunities which would
have occurred by remaining in their usual quarters.

St. Bernard passed the remainder of the year at
Spires, and did not resume his homeward journey
till the 4th January, 1145. At his departure, the

emperor, the princes, and numerous battalions of
Crusaders crowded around, to hear his gentle words
for the last time, and offer him every testimony of
veneration and respect.

He addressed to them a touching adieu, and his
words, says his historian, " were more like divine
than human." Bernard descended the Rhine to
Cologne, where·he knew the inhabitants were anxious to receive him; and when the news of his
arrival became known in the city, the people flocked
in crowds to his dwelling, and testified their rejoicing through the whole night. The crowd was so
close, and so intolerable, says the historian, " that
the holy Abbot could not go out of the house."
He remained at a window, from which he blessed
the people, and it was only by means of a ladder,
placed in the street, that they were able to present
the sick to his notice, whom he restored to health
by his prayers. They dared not open the doors on
account of the multitude which besieged the entrance.
"As to myself," said the monk, Gerard, " being
desirous of entering the house, I could not do so in
any way; and from nine in the morning I remained
in the street until the evening, without being able
either to reach the door or the ladder, so completely
was every avenue stopped up."

George. Why, Grandmamma, had St. Bernard been
the Emperor Conrad, they could not have done him
greater honour.

Grandmamma. St. Bernard, my child, was the
humble follower of Him who said that " His kingdom was not of this world." The more he despised
honours, the more anxious were the people to thrust
them upon him. The Emperor Conrad's name is
forgotten by thousands, to whom that of St. Bernard
has become a household word. Many sick people

were restored to health by St. Bernard's prayers, during his stay in Cologne; and on the sixth of February he returned to Clairvaux, broken in health, and crowned with the glory of the numberless good works he had performed since he had last left its peaceful roof.

_____

CHAPTER VI.

Elizabeth. Will you finish the history of St. Bernard, this morning, Grandmamma? It is too wet for us to go out, and George has not yet done his drawing. It would be very nice if you could tell us the story, while we are preparing for the drawing-master.

George. I should like to have a print of Clairvaux to copy, and a head of St. Bernard, in his habit.

Grandmamma. Better learn to copy his favourite oaks and beech trees, my little boy; recollect the lesson they taught him, and remember that it was studying God's works that made him the exemplary Christian he became. But let us return to him. In the spring of this year, 1147, Pope Eugenius the Third, who, you remember, was that quiet, humble brother who lit the stoves at Clairvaux, arrived in France; King Louis the Seventh went to meet him as far as Dijon, and they returned to St. Denis together, where they arrived on Easter eve. All the principal Crusaders assisted at the religious ceremonies the following day; among them were one hundred Knights of the Temple, with their Grand Master at their head. The French force amounted to 100,000 men, and that of the Emperor

Conrad was not less numerous. This vast army set
out on the 29th June 1147, two months after the
Germans. Disasters without parallel followed them,
and about two years afterwards King Louis returned from the Holy Land, accompanied by a few
hundred knights, the sad and sickly remains of that
gallant Christian force, which had left France so
full of hope, so certain of victory.

George. Why, Grandmamma, what became of
them all?

Grandmamma. Some died in battle, some of the
plague, many of hunger, and more of fatigue; there
was scarcely a family in France without some loss to
deplore. The country was almost ruined. The
nobles had mortgaged their property to Jews and
money-lenders, to enable them to get money for the
heavy expenses of such an expedition. The peasants
had followed their chiefs to the war; the fields were
uncultivated, the government was without resources.
These unlooked for events fell heavily on the tender heart of St. Bernard. He felt that he has stir-
red up France to the unlucky war in Palestine; that
he had preached the crusade, and thus was one
means of bringing these disasters upon his country.
St. Bernard wrote his "Apology," in which he
shows them that if they had conducted themselves
like Christians in this war, that is, loyally and
piously, God would not have abandoned their cause;
but as they gave themselves up to all sorts of
crimes, the Almighty withdrew His support from
them. Another sorrow came about the same time,
to diminish the little strength which still enabled
our great Saint to fulfil his duties at Clairvaux—it
was the death of his disciple, Pope Eugenius, who
expired after a short illness, on the 8th July, 1153.
St. Bernard wept bitterly at this unexpected news,

and became more and more indifferent to everything belonging to this world. He was too weak to leave his bed, and his poor monks were hourly expecting to be summoned to witness his death, but a last miracle was to illustrate St. Bernard's departure from this earth, he could not die like the generality of the poor sinners with which it is peopled.

George. Is he really going to die?· I am so sorry for it; I quite love St. Bernard.

Grandmamma. Yes, my little boy, we have arrived very near to the last scene, but there is a curious and striking effort to do good for the last time, which I must recount to you.

The Archbishop of Treves came to Clairvaux to entreat our great Christian hero to assist in pacifying the province of Metz, where the nobles and the common people were killing each other; already 2,000 persons had perished.

At this affecting recital St. Bernard sat up in his bed; his muscles seemed to receive fresh strength; despite the entreaties of his brethren he determined to go to Metz, and suddenly, to the astonishment of both armies, the dying St. Bernard appeared between them, supported and carried by some of the monks of Clairvaux. Too feeble to make his voice heard, he was taken from one camp to the other, and though the leaders were unwilling at first to listen to his arguments, yet in the night they sent a deputation to say they would accept his mediation. The next day he assembled them all on a little island in the river. St. Bernard's voice, so weak in tone, so powerful in argument, once more triumphed over the fiery passions of wicked men, and he left Metz with the consoling assurance that he had brought peace where he had found war.

St. Bernard again returned to his beloved Clair-

vaux. The strength which he had so suddenly
acquired as suddenly left him, and he was laid on
his narrow bed from which he was only removed to
be carried to his grave. His children stood around
him, while tears rolled down many furrowed cheeks,
and many an aged monk grieved as they never
thought to grieve again. "Oh! kind, good father,
will you then leave this monastery? Have you no
pity upon us your poor children, whom you have
brought up like a tender parent? What will become
of us, whom you have loved so well?" These
piteous words moved the heart of the dying Saint,
and he wept.

"I know not to which I ought to yield, the love
of my children which urges me to stay here, or the
love of my God, which draws me to Him."

These were his last words.

The tolling of the bells of Clairvaux, and the
funeral services, entoned by 700 monks, announced
to the world the death of the great and good St.
Bernard. It took place on the 20th of August,
1153, about nine in the morning. He was sixty-
three years of age, and had been consecrated to God's
service for forty years, during thirty-eight of which
he had exercised the functions of an abbot. By all
subsequent ages he has been regarded as one of the
brightest lights of the Christian Church. His
writings were one of her surest bulwarks, and his
pious and useful life was a practical example of the
excellence of his maxims.

George. I am so sorry that he died. But what
became of his brother, who went with him so young
to the monastery? I mean little Nivard.

Grandmamma. History does not mention him.
Probably he lived at Clairvaux until it pleased God
to take him to rejoin St. Bernard. When people lead

such good lives, my dear little boy, they look forward to death with pleasure, for they know that God will take them from the sickness and sorrow of this world, to that holy peace and joy which He has prepared in Heaven for those who have obeyed His commandments on earth.

May such be your fate, my children, and such it will certainly be, if you try to imitate his virtues, and follow the two great rules of his life.

Love God and your neighbour.